The Reflection

AUTHOR:
HELÉNA MACALINO

ILLUSTRATOR:
JUSTYNA PAWLUCZUK

CRYSTAL
MOSAIC
BOOKS

THE REFLECTION

Text and layout by Heléna Macalino
Copyright© 2014
Illustrated by Justyna Pawluczuk

For information, address Crystal Mosaic Books,
PO Box 1276 Hillsboro, OR 97123
ISBN: 978-0-9911061-6-5

DEDICATED TO THE PEOPLE I LOVE.

Get Your Free Book!

Join the Super Secret Reader List and get a free copy of

The Wish Fish Activity Book

part of The Wish Fish Early Reader Series.

Super Secret Readers get free books, posters, videos, and all kinds of other great goodies, so hop on over to
www.macalino.com
and sign up today!

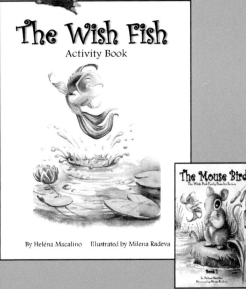

The adventure has just begun!

Once upon a time, a girl named
Meltha walked down a path.
She saw a puddle.

She saw the reflection of the garden.

She stepped in the puddle.

She fell in.

She landed in
a mysterious
garden.

Bunny guards stood
beneath an oak tree.

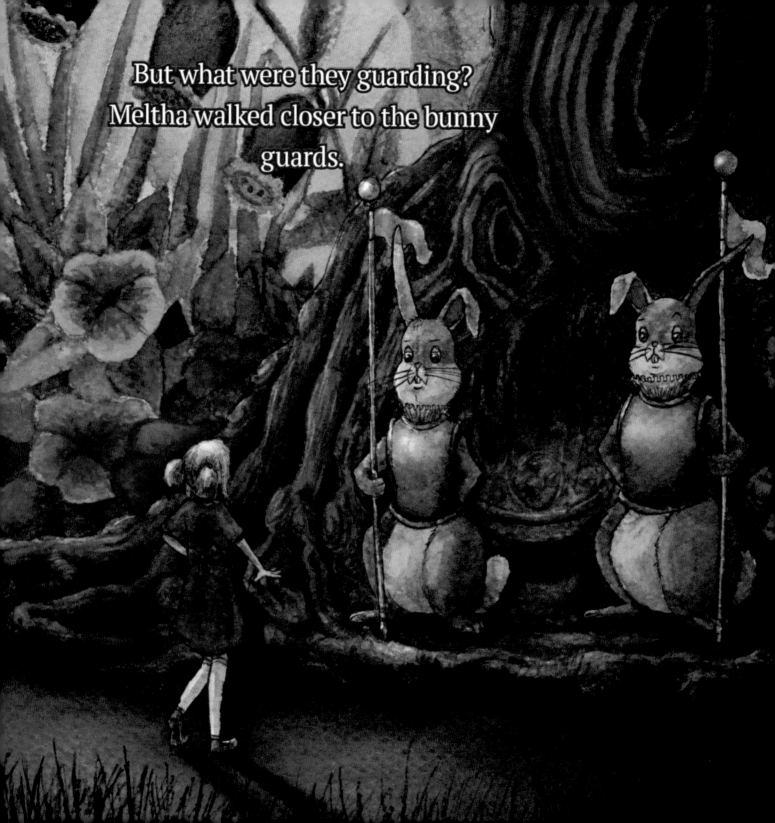

But what were they guarding?
Meltha walked closer to the bunny
guards.

She saw a gate.

The bunnies opened the gate.
Meltha walked in.

The bunnies closed the
gate behind her.

At first there was nothing.

Steps appeared.
She followed the steps to
the top.

When she got to the top,
the stairs disappeared.
She found herself in a little
room. It was dark.

She reached her hands into a corner. Something crawled onto her hand. She yelped.

But it was not a spider.
It was a rope.

When she tried to climb it, it opened a secret door.

Meltha blinked. Sand covered her shoes.

She walked onto a mysterious island
surrounded by water.

Monkey guards stood beneath
coconut trees.
"I want to go home."

The monkeys opened the door. Meltha covered her eyes and walked in.

Her cat said "Perrow?"

Once upon a time, a girl named Ahtlem walked down a garden path.

She saw a puddle.

Get Your Free Book!

Join the Super Secret Reader List and get a free copy of

The Wish Fish Activity Book

part of The Wish Fish Early Reader Series.

Super Secret Readers get free books, posters, videos, and all kinds of other great goodies, so hop on over to

www.macalino.com

and sign up today!

Don't let the adventure end!

Author: Heléna Macalino

Heléna is a 2nd grader living in Portland, OR with her family, two kittens, and two hamsters (and if she had her way, a couple of horses, some guinea pigs, a pair of dogs... and definitely a bunny). Heléna loves art and mysterious stories involving animals.
So she wrote one!

Illustrator: Justyna Pawluczuk

Justyna is an illustrator specializing in traditional media. She is currently living in Warsaw, Poland. Her goal is to bring the best of the worlds of classic and modern illustration. While not honing her skills she enjoys a good book or is planning her next hiking trip.

You can reach Justyna at:
http://justynapawluczuk.daportfolio.com/
pawluczukjustyna@gmail.com

Made in the USA
Columbia, SC
20 November 2019